This Little Hippo
book belongs to:

Scholastic Children's Books,
Commonwealth House, 1-19 New Oxford Street,
London WC1A 1NU, UK
a division of Scholastic Ltd

London - New York - Toronto - Sydney - Auckland
Mexico City - New Delhi - Hong Kong

First published by Scholastic Ltd, 1999

Developed from the
original books by Michelle Cartlidge.
Story adapted by Caryn Jenner. Illustrated by Colin Twinn.
2 4 6 8 10 9 7 5 3 1

ISBN 0 590 11376 3

Printed in China

Michelle Cartlidge's

TEDDY TRUCKS

Gerry the Star

Little
Hippo

One evening, the Teddy Truck drivers met at Rosie's Café after work.

"You all look very smart!" Rosie told them.

"We're going to see the Ballet Rumbear," said Bella.

"I didn't know you liked ballet dancing," said Rosie.

"Wilson says we'll like it," said Jacko. "I'm not so sure."

In the Teddy Trucks office, Boss Bear and Dusty were looking forward to the ballet that evening.

"Mrs Boss Bear can't come with us tonight," Boss Bear told Dusty. "She's not well."

"Oh dear," said Dusty.

BRRRING! BRRRING!

"Perhaps Mrs Boss Bear is better!" said Boss Bear, as he picked up the telephone. But it was the director of the Ballet Rumbear. "Certainly. Teddy Trucks can help," Boss Bear told him.

Boss Bear phoned Rosie's Café right away.

"I'll tell them," said Rosie. She put down the telephone. "Boss Bear needs a driver to make an urgent delivery."

"I'll go!" said Jacko.

"It's your turn to buy the ice creams at the theatre," said Wilson.

"I'd do it," offered Gerry. "But I'd miss the ballet."

"Don't worry. The ballet won't start until you deliver the costumes," said Rosie.

11

Gerry drove to the depot to collect the costumes.

The porter ticked his list as Gerry loaded the costumes on to his truck.

"That's the lot," said the porter at last. "Deliver the costumes to the Grand Theatre. They're very late."

"Don't worry," called Gerry, jumping into the cab. "Leave it to Teddy Trucks!"

The Grand Theatre was crowded. Lots of teddies wanted to see the famous Ballet Rumbear.

"I hope Gerry gets here in time," said Boss Bear.

BALLET RUMBEAR

"I'm sure he will," said Dusty. "The dancers need their costumes!"

"They could leap about in vests," Jacko laughed.

"Jacko, you'll like ballet," said Wilson. "I know it."

TICKETS

15

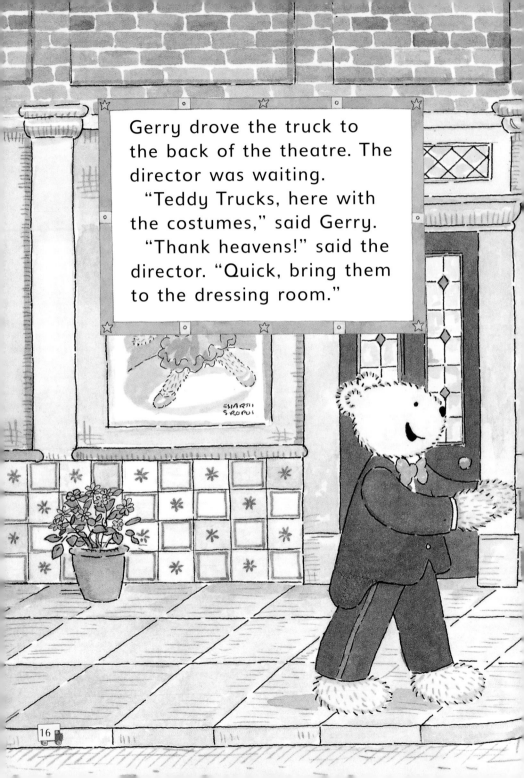

Gerry drove the truck to the back of the theatre. The director was waiting.

"Teddy Trucks, here with the costumes," said Gerry.

"Thank heavens!" said the director. "Quick, bring them to the dressing room."

As soon as the dancers saw their costumes, they hurried to put them on.

"Can you hold this for me, please?" asked the director. He put a sparkly crown on Gerry's head.

"And this," said a dancer.
"This, too," said another.
Soon, Gerry was holding a
pile of costumes.

"Excuse me," he said, but the director didn't hear.

"Right!" called the director. "Everyone on stage. Hurry! Curtain up!"

He led the dancers out of the dressing room.

Rehearsa
Monday
Tuesday
Wednesday
Thursday
Friday

Gerry was left by himself with the pile of costumes. He went into the corridor.

"Don't you need these costumes?" he asked.

But the director and the dancers were rushing about.

Gerry heard clapping and
then the music began. At
last, he found the director
standing behind the curtain.

"Excuse me," he said.

The director saw the crown
on Gerry's head. "The prince
is here! You're just in time."
He took the extra costumes.
"You won't need these for
the first scene." Then he
gave Gerry a little push.

Suddenly, Gerry found himself on the stage!
All around him, dancers leapt and twirled to the music. A ballerina in a pink tutu leapt into Gerry's arms, then twirled out again.

Gerry didn't know what to do. He decided to join in. He tried a little hop for himself. Then a big leap and a twirl. What fun!

"Is that Gerry?" Boss Bear gasped from the audience.
   Gerry's friends watched in amazement as he danced with the ballerinas. The Teddy Truck drivers were speechless.

The dancers danced off stage, leaving Gerry alone in front of the crowd. He gave one more leap and a spectacular twirl before the music finished.

The audience clapped and cheered loudly for the Ballet Rumbear. Some people threw flowers on to the stage for the star of the show.

Gerry took a deep bow. Jacko clapped especially hard. "I guess you were right, Wilson," he laughed. "I did like the ballet."